THIS WALKER BOOK BELONGS TO:

BOY COOK FISHERMAN CLOWN

Written by
PAUL MANNING

Illustrated by
NICOLA BAYLEY

WALKER BOOKS
LONDON

First published 1987 by Walker Books Ltd
87 Vauxhall Walk, London SE11 5HJ
as *Clown*, *Cook*, *Boy* and *Fisherman*

This edition published 1990

Text © 1987 Paul Manning
Illustrations © 1987 Nicola Bayley

Printed in Hong Kong by
Sheck Wah Tong Printing Press Ltd

British Library Cataloguing in Publication Data
Manning, Paul
Merry-go-Rhymes.
I. Title   II. Bayley, Nicola
821'.914   PZ8.3
ISBN 0-7445-1296-4

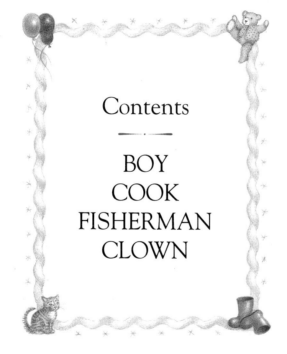

Contents

Early
morning,
boy
yawning.

Bad luck,
head stuck.

Boy
slopping,
cup
dropping.

Clothes
drying,
boy
crying.

Sister
pushing,
boy
whooshing.

On the rug,
nice and
snug.

Father
washing,
boy
sploshing.

Sleepyhead,
time
for bed.

Who's that
in the big
white
hat?

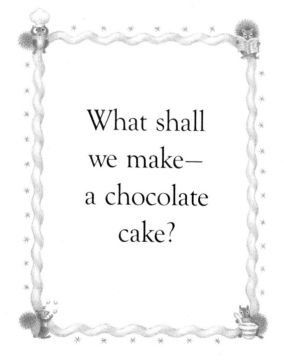

What shall
we make—
a chocolate
cake?

Three, four…
a spoonful
more.

Slop,
splatter,
mix the
batter.

Sticky paste,

try a taste.

Cook looking,
how's it
cooking?

Bang, bong,
sound the
gong.

What's
for tea?
Look
and see!

FISHERMAN

Heave ho!
Away we
go.

Rub-a-dub,
scour
and
scrub.

Net's full,
tug and
pull.

Lower
the catch,
down
the hatch.

Mind
that plate—
too late!

Achooo!
Wet
through.

Prepare
the buoy.
Land ahoy!

Heave
a sigh,
home
and dry.

CLOWN

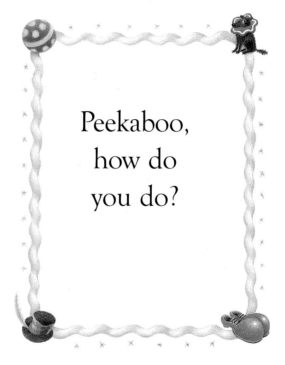

Peekaboo,
how do
you do?

Quick, slow,
catch and
throw.

Clip, clop,
jump on
top.

Careful,
clown,
don't look
down!

Trip,
stumble,
take a
tumble.

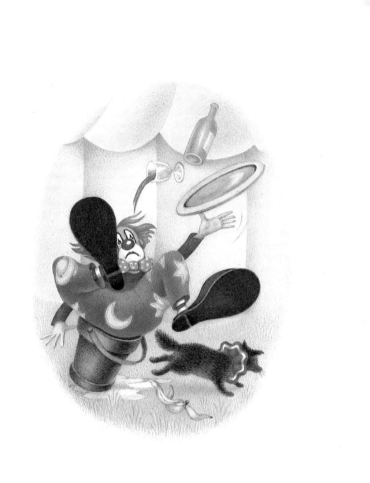

Poor hat—
squashed
flat!

I spy...
a
custard
pie!

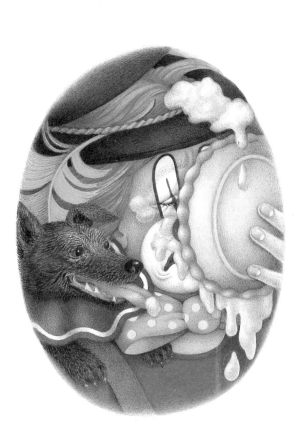

Take a bow,
that's all
for now.

NICOLA BAYLEY'S BEDTIME RHYMES
NICOLA BAYLEY'S NONSENSE RHYMES

Two wonderfully illustrated collections of twelve
favourite poems – each ideal for reading aloud.

"The lullabies are perfect for rocking little ones to
sleep, the nonsense rhymes provoke plenty of early
morning giggles and the illustrations to them
all are minutely detailed."
Young Mother

"Beautifully detailed and finely executed paintings."
Books For Keeps

NICOLA BAYLEY'S COPYCATS

Five delightful feline fantasies.

"Exquisite little fantasies…
The miniature lushness which spills out from each
page is as captivating to the adult as to the child."
The Times Educational Supplement

"A must to collect and keep."
Options

*Spider Cat • Parrot Cat • Elephant Cat
Crab Cat • Polar Bear Cat*

MORE WALKER PAPERBACKS

For You to Enjoy

NICOLA BAYLEY'S
COPYCATS

Spider Cat	ISBN 0-7445-1205-0
Crab Cat	ISBN 0-7445-1206-9
Elephant Cat	ISBN 0-7445-1207-7
Polar Bear Cat	ISBN 0-7445-1208-5
Parrot Cat	ISBN 0-7445-1209-3

£1.99 each

Nicola Bayley's Bedtime Rhymes	ISBN 0-7445-1324-3
Nicola Bayley's Nonsense Rhymes	ISBN 0-7445-1323-5

£1.99 each